Samuel French Acting Edition

The Arsonists

by Jacqueline Goldfinger

SAMUELFRENCH.COM   SAMUELFRENCH.CO.UK

FOR PRODUCTION ENQUIRIES

UNITED STATES AND CANADA
Info@SamuelFrench.com
1-866-598-8449

UNITED KINGDOM AND EUROPE
Plays@SamuelFrench.co.uk
020-7255-4302

Each title is subject to availability from Samuel French, depending
upon country of performance. Please be aware that THE ARSONISTS
may not be licensed by Samuel French in your territory. Professional
and amateur producers should contact the nearest Samuel French
office or licensing partner to verify availability.

MUSIC USE NOTE

Licensees are solely responsible for obtaining formal written permission from copyright owners to use copyrighted music in the performance of this play and are strongly cautioned to do so. If no such permission is obtained by the licensee, then the licensee must use only original music that the licensee owns and controls. Licensees are solely responsible and liable for all music clearances and shall indemnify the copyright owners of the play(s) and their licensing agent, Samuel French, against any costs, expenses, losses and liabilities arising from the use of music by licensees. Please contact the appropriate music licensing authority in your territory for the rights to any incidental music.

IMPORTANT BILLING AND CREDIT REQUIREMENTS

If you have obtained performance rights to this title, please refer to your licensing agreement for important billing and credit requirements.

THE ARSONISTS had a rolling world premiere through the National New Play Network's RWP Program (Nan Barnett, Executive Director; Jordana Fraider, Programs). It premiered at four theaters in one year:

RWP produced by Azuka Theatre: Kevin Glaccum, producing artistic director; Allison Heishman, director; Sally Ollove, dramaturg; Dirk Durossette, scenic designer; J. Dominic Chacon, lighting designer; Becca Austin, costume designer; Andrew Nelson, sound designer; Alisa Sickora Kleckner, FX makeup designer; Avista Custom Theatrical, properties; Joe Daniels, technical director; Terry Mittleman, stage manager; Lauren Tracy, production manager; Bianca Canosa, assistant stage manager. The cast was as follows:

M..Sarah Gliko
H...Steven Rishard

RWP produced by Capital Stage: Michael Stevenson, artistic director; Gail Dartez, director; Brian Harrower, scenic & lighting design; Mari Carson, Costumes. The cast was as follows:

M.. Megan Wicks
H... Rich Hebert

RWP produced by Perseverance Theatre: Art Rotch, artistic director and director; Anne Szeliski, stage manager; Sara Ryung Clement, sets; Lauren Mckenzie Miller, lights; Elizabeth Rocha, costumes. The cast was as follows:

M...Allison Holtkamp
H...Aaron Elmore

RWP produced by Know Theatre: Andrew J. Hungerford, artistic director and scenic & lighting designer; Tamara Winters, director; Noelle Johnson, costume design; Doug Borntrager, sound design; Sarah Beth Hall, scenic art & prop design. The cast was as follows:

M.. Erin Ward
H...Jim Stark

CHARACTERS

M – twenties, female, any race, plays guitar, sings a little
H – fifties, male, any race, plays guitar, sings a little
*M and H should feel like family.

SETTING

Empty family cabin, a stripped wooden legacy

TIME

1990s, Florida Swamp

AUTHOR'S NOTES

Music

This is not a musical, however, there are a few moments of musicality between the father and daughter. All referenced music is American traditional and in the public domain. The required music is located in the back of the book.

Accent

The North Florida accent has a Southern cadence and softness but no heavy twang or drawn-out speech. Space should only be left between words and phrases when it will mean something.

Production Note

At one point, a character chops a floor with an ax. This can be easily done with a false floor and one plank of wood that's replaced every night.

Runtime

Eighty minutes, no intermission.

Special Thanks to Edward Sobel, Cristina Alicea, Allison Heishman, Nan Barnett, The Kennedy Center's Page-to-Stage Program, and Unexpected Stage Company.

This is a love letter to my father.

He is not dead.

It's a shame that folks hold off 'til somebody dies to say how much they mean to 'em.

I'm gonna go ahead and do it now.

1. Cabin

(1990s, Florida Swamp.)

(Dim lights rise.)

(A rough plank floor cradles a beat-up guitar, a long-standing cardboard box.)

(Sound of powerboat motor.)

(Sound of banging and dragging.)

(Sound of under-breath cursing and heaving.)

(The door slams open.)

(M, daughter, screams from offstage.)

M. *(Offstage.)* Goddamn motherfucker.

(M enters.)

(She wears a singed flannel shirt, men's work pants, work boots, large dirty hikers, backpack with wooden tools sticking out.)

(She lugs a white cloth bag that blood seeps through.)

(She slams the door closed, drops the bag, breathes heavily.)

(Sound of police siren in the distance.)

Goddamn motherfuckers.

(Pulls ax out of backpack.)

Mother mother mother...

(Begins chopping floorboards.)

Mother mother...

(Floorboards splinter.)

Mother mother...

(Sirens and splintering.)

M. Mother mother mother mother...

> *(Sirens and splintering and holding back tears.)*

Mother mother mother mother mother mother mother mother mother mother mother mother mother...

> *(A fierce refusal to cry.)*
>
> *(Sirens.)*
>
> *(She drops the ax, pries up floorboards.)*
>
> *(She drags white, blood-soaked bag to hole.)*
>
> *(She stands over hole with bag. She can't push it in. She can't. Can't, can't, can't, just can't.)*
>
> *(Sound of deafening siren.)*
>
> *(She can't do it, won't do it.)*
>
> *(Sound of deafening siren and police lights flashing outside.)*
>
> *(She leans over the hole. Touches her fingers to her lips, kisses them, touches her fingers to the hole. A moment of prayer, a sign of grace.)*
>
> *(She quickly shoves the bag into the hole in the floor, replaces floorboards.)*
>
> *(She turns light off, hides in corner.)*
>
> *(She waits.)*
>
> *(She waits, tries not to breathe, refuses to cry.)*
>
> *(She bites back fear until it returns to rage.)*
>
> *(The sound of a police car driving away, a retreating siren.)*

Motherfuckers.

> *(She dumps the tools with a clatter and kneels down next to the plank-covered hole.)*

...

...

(She kisses her fingers, touches her fingers to the planks.)

…

(She stands, strips out of the work clothes like shedding skin, throws them in a corner, rummages through the cardboard box, pulls out a denim dress, slips it on.)

(Pulls out a distinctively 1970s coat which is at odds with her nineties look, puts it on.)

(To hole.) I will never forgive you.

…

(Picks up guitar, strums.)

…

(Begins to play and sing the American traditional tune "Raleigh and Spencer.")

RALEIGH AND SPENCER ARE BURNING DOWN
THERE AIN'T NO MORE LIQUOR IN THIS TOWN
THERE AIN'T NO MORE LIQUOR IN THIS TOWN
I'LL PAWN YOU MY SHOES FOR A BOTTLE OF BOOZE
I'LL DRINK IT AND I'LL LAY RIGHT DOWN AND DIE
I'LL DRINK IT AND I'LL LAY RIGHT DOWN AND DIE
RALEIGH AND SPENCER ARE BURNING DOWN
THERE AIN'T NO MORE LIQUOR IN THIS TOWN
THERE AIN'T NO MORE LIQUOR IN THIS TOWN
YOU CAN TROMP DOWN THE FIRES THAT GROW AROUND
  MY GRAVE

M & H. *(H offstage.)*
THEY'LL RISE

H. *(Rises from hole in floor.)*
AND BLOOM AGAIN
THEY'LL RISE AND BLOOM AGAIN.

(M is struck silent.)

(H, father, crawls out of the hole, a little bloody but intact. This is not how she put him down there.)

H. Hey Littles.

M. …

   …

   …

H. It's okay.

   It's just me.

   (Regarding coat.)

   Your momma's skin never fit quite right, did it?

M. …

H. *(Regarding outside.)* You didn't have to try to burn them all.

   Coulda set a shorter lead.

M. They got you.

H. They didn't get me, Littles.

   I got me.

   You got me.

M. They got you.

   An' I got 'em back.

H. Please.

   Happens sometimes.

   The wind blows the wrong way.

   The ground drier than you think.

   (Snaps fingers.)

   Goes up.

   Flames bite faster than dogs.

   Perils of the –

M. Never before.

H. Your grandfather, for one.

   A great-uncle, for another.

   Flames fed by family for years back.

   Happens sometimes.

M. Never to you.

H. Until now.

M. I saw you...

H. I know.

M. Burn.

    I saw you,

    Fall and...

    I covered you with my body.

    ...

H. Let's not, I can't remember.

    ...

    Not too much.

M. You were in flames.

    And then you were out.

    And then gone.

    No breath,

    It's like the wind through the pines drew it off you,

    Left you in charred pieces.

    And sirens jumped up,

    From around...

    They hurled at me.

    So I sopped a gasoline line and lit another fire,

    Turned it their way.

    A wall of flames to shield,

    Brought you home.

H. You shoulda left –

M. Fuck you!

    Shoulda left you?

    Left to burn? Left to rot into ash? Left to –

H. Fire woulda killed all the evidence.

    You'da been safer, Doodlebug.

M. You're a fucking asshole.

       (Runs to him.)

       (They embrace lovingly.)

       (Pushes her face into his work shirt.)

(Breathes in deeply.)

M. *(Low.)* I hate you.

    (Holds him tighter.)

You left me.

H. Come now.

Come on.

    *(**H** releases **M**.)*

Aren't you gonna ask why –

M. Don't care.

But now that you're back,

I've got to do. We've got to do.

Clean up.

Disposal.

Get rid of the stray fuses.

Wash our clothes.

The Police already drove past.

Right past.

H. They may have seen your face,

When you took your time to collect me.

M. They never figure.

H. Might.

I can't read the wind today.

M. They gone.

H. You need to get me outta here, Littles.

I'm proof.

…

Clean up.

…

Disposal.

…

Littles.

M. No.

(**M** *cleans up from fire.*)

H. I want you to take me outta here.

M. ...

   ...

   ...

H. Don't make that face.

M. It's your face.

H. That must be why I don't like it.
It's all –

M. I don't care. You're here, that's all I –

H. It's not natural.

M. What you know from natural?

H. The Maker spit me back out, Littles.
You know why?

M. You always said, we make it look natural.
God's just jealous.
He can't set a fire, make it look as natural as we do.
We fool better than Him.

H. Because I'm incomplete.
Because there's a part ah me you missed, back at the fire.
That you left between the smoke and the air, the fire and the grass.
What's left of life in the in-betweens.
The breath between my bones escaped,
But the bones themselves are holy and the earth is calling them home.
There's some piece of me left out there.

M. Please.

H. You got to go back, Littles.
You got to collect me all, put me in the ground all together.
Otherwise, I can't ascend.

M. We might descend.

H. We might.

> (**M** *gets orange from box.*)
>
> (*Tosses one to* **H.**)

The dead don't eat.

M. (*Peels it.*) (*Eats.*) Good. Save us money.
We're not gonna get paid for this fire.
This one turned into a real mess.

H. You'll get paid.
You set it. It burned.

M. Bad luck all night round.

...

Think he'll get the insurance money?

H. Should.
But customers don't like to pay for a mess.
And that one was as messy as it gets.

M. Then I'm real glad you're not hungry because that's my
last orange.

H. (*Tosses orange back to* **M.**) ...

...

You know, Littles,
I seen a tiger once.
Right here, off our dock.

> (**M** *peels, eats orange and listens to a good tall
> tale.*)

M. Liar.
No tigers in Florida.
Panthers.

H. I did. I saw one.
He was lounging too.

M. (*As in "sure, yeah, right."*) I hear.

H. Loungin' out beside the water.
Right next to where the dock meets the land.
Walking through the high grass.

M. Can't see nothin' in that grass.

H. Can so, if it's a tiger.

   They big damn animals.

M. *(Clicks tongue.)* Cats don't swim neither.

H. This 'un does.

   Hush now, it's my story.

> (**M** *peels the other orange, eats, listens.*)

On the dock.

Near my boat.

In the tall grass.

Which, yes, I can see through.

That tiger was golden orange an' black stripes, thick an' strong. With a tail, too.

M. *(Mouth full.)* Uh-huh.

H. You'd like tigers, Littles.

   Tigers always in flames. Stripes shimmer,

   Just with the walkin' of it. An' when it runs,

   Shit,

   Looks like fire spreadin' through the trees.

   Tall pines, from soil to sky, row on row on row, with this streak of fire runnin' through it, leavin' nothin' behind.

   No smoke.

   No ashes.

   The cleanest burn you ever seen.

   The tiger's the best controlled burn.

   You'd be jealous ah that Littles.

   Even you with a hun'red packs ah matches couldn't do that.

   Burn so clean you leave nothin' behind.

M. You hadn't ever seen no tiger,

   On no dock,

   In Florida.

H. I did.

   An' there he be.

On fire standin' still.

...

You can't be a tiger, Littles, all heat an' power an' control.

You can't control the fire that good.

Neither can I.

Whether it be the fire,

Or the heat,

Or the police,

Or the sheer weight of time,

There's always somethin' more than you, Littles.

Somethin' out of your control.

...

...

The wind kicks up –

M. I'm tired of this.

H. It kicks at the moment I light the head fuse.

It catches my hand and wrist collar.

Jump cross my arms, melts the buttons –

M. Don't need to hear –

H. From my,

...

At, when, at that, when it jumped,

'Cross my body. That's when I knew it.

And I look across the field at you,

Just,

Doin', what I taught you,

Just, shinin' in our own light.

I knew you's ready. And I knew I's done.

I said goodbye to you then, Littles.

You couldn't get 'cross that field in time unless you flew.

And that's one I couldn't teach.

What you can do now,

Put me in the ground, give me peace.

Leave.

Start somethin' new.

You can control that.

You got a tiger by the tail, Doodlebug.

You think you own it now, but that's a trick.

It already owns you.

You don't get out, it'll take what it wants in the end.

M. ...

...

You talk like,

...

You talk like,

McCabe and Mrs. Miller.

H. You too little to see that movie,

Littles.

You too young to wear that coat,

To wear our lives around you until it squeezes yours out.

M. Personal weakness.

You said the movie, it was about personal weakness.

What keeps us in tatters about the place.

And you found a,

Way around,

A fountain of youth.

H. At a cost.

M. So buck the fuck up.

You fine.

H. I can't go.

I can't leave this house.

You have to go for me.

You have to find the rest of me, bring it back, bury me together.

Then I'll rest.

M. Too much work to rest now, Daddy.

(**M** *picks up floorboard on opposite site of room.*)

(**H** *picks up guitar and strums quietly.*)

(**M** *pulls twine, fuses, and other arson tools up from the floorboards.*)

H. How's the count now?

M. Two fuses needed for next week.
Seven the week after.
Handful of extra for whatever.

H. Don't take no short-order jobs.
Hasty fires not well set.
Fires people don't know if they really want yet,
Make trouble.

M. *(Re: their predicament.)* Nor non-hasty ones, sometimes.

H. *(Strums.)* ...
...
...

(**M** *sits to make new fuses.*)

(**M** *rolls out long lines of multi-colored twine and string across the length of the stage, or perhaps strings them over a rafter.*)

(*Initially,* **M** *rolls out the lines of twine neatly, but when* **H** *looks away she twists the twine; intentionally messes up her work.*)

(**H** *points out various places in the rows of twine that are caught up.*)

(Strums.) Keep straight.
There.
There, Littles. There.

(**M** *moves to those places, fixes the twine.*)

M. See, what I do without you.

H. *(He's not stupid.)* You been layin' that right since you was eight.

M. I don't know what you're talkin' 'bout.

(But she does, he does. The poor deception is
an act of gentle desperation.)

H. *(Keeps playing guitar.)*
(Re: the twine rows.) Our fertile fields.

M. Rows rows rows.

(**H** *strums the opening notes to the American*
traditional tune "Poor Wayfaring Stranger"
on the guitar.)

(**M** *recognizes them, suppresses a smile, then*
a laugh. She knows he's trying to manipulate
her and it's not going to work.)

(**H** *thinks this might have a long shot.)*

(**H** *plays and sings as she begins braiding the*
twine together.)

H.

I AM A POOR WAYFARING STRANGER
WHILE TRAV'LING THRU THIS WORLD OF WOE,
YET THERE'S NO SICKNESS, TOIL NOR DANGER
IN THAT BRIGHT WORLD TO WHICH I GO.
I'M GOING THERE TO SEE MY MOTHER,
I'M GOING THERE NO MORE TO ROAM.
I'M ONLY GOING OVER JORDAN,
I'M ONLY GOING OVER HOME.
LET ME GO UP OVER HOME.
LET ME GO, UP OVER, HOME.

M. *(Indicates twine.)* A deception just as poor as messin'
with the rows.
I've got no sympathy.

H. Couldn't hurt to try.

M. This is your home.

H. Littles.

M. Useless to say otherwise.

H. Weakness sometimes masquerades as strength.

M. Throw me a costume party.

H. These are like all those times

I told your mother we should spank you.

M. You did once.

H. Yes, ma'am, I did.

M. *(Toying with him.)* And how'd that go?

H. ...

Just made you worse.

> *(The first row of twine fuses has been braided together in a tight rope.)*

M. Yes, sir, it did.

Come on and help now.

> *(**H** nods. Stands. Winces in pain. Doesn't drop the guitar, though.)*

Daddy?

H. ...

...

...

Nothing.

M. It's your side.

H. Go get the bucket.

M. I'm not –

H. You can keep me here, Littles.

I might even,

Want you to,

A speck.

But just a speck.

This middle, it's torture, not being one way or the other.

I feel my insides churning out.

> *(They embrace.)*

M. I'll hold you together.

H. *(Warning.)* Tigers, Littles.

...

...

...

...

...

...

...

(*H's pain resolves.*)

(*M pulls the bucket out of the cardboard box.*)

(*Together they dip the long, newly braided fuse into a concoction in the bucket, squeeze out the excess, and hang it from the ceiling to dry. If the braided fuses are already hanging, they take an old cloth, soak it in the bucket, and squeeze and rub the liquid into the hanging fuses.*)

(*They start on another row of twine. H and M work together in perfect tandem. It's like the old days.*)

(*They share inside jokes and make faces.*)

(*They start and stop a hymn or two.*)

(*Their life is vertical, in-place, right again.*)

(*It's a moment of pure love.*)

(*This goes on for a while.*)

(*This the last golden moment on this last golden day that neither wants ever to end.*)

(*By the end of the moments, a long, porous curtain of twine hangs across the cabin.*)

(*Lights shift.*)

2. Cabin

(**M** *sleeps.*)

(**H** *checks hanging fuses.*)

(*Some are dry enough to cut into varying lengths for fuses.*)

(*Some are still too wet.*)

(*He checks and measures and cuts as if he was born to, as if this is the only thing he's ever known how to do and he wouldn't do anything else. Clean, smooth, lithe, and beautiful.*)

(*Throughout the scene they cut fuses to differing lengths, so that the fuse curtain is slowly cut away.*)

H. Clotho.

Lachesis.

Atropos.

Spinner.

Measurer.

Cutter of the thread.

Who said that?

Who said that now.

Grandfather?

...

Great Uncle...?

Clotho Spinner.

Lachesis Measurer.

Atropos Cutter.

Damn Greeks.

Spin Measure Cut. Spin Measure Cut. Spin Measure Cut. Spin Measure Cut.

Spin Measure Cut. Spin Measure –

Who...[said that]?

(**M** *wakes slowly, sleepily.*)

H & M. Spin Measure Cut.

Spin Measure Cut.

Spin Measure –

M. Make sure you give me a coupla long 'uns.

Maybe half the room length.

H. Who said,

Littles,

Who said,

Clotho. Lachesis. Atropos.

The spinner.

The measurer.

The cutter.

M. Cousin Need.

H. The short one?

M. The skinny one.

The one that read all that Truman Capote all the time.

H. You sure?

M. Yeah.

(**H** *stands frozen.*)

(**H** *looks at hands.*)

(*What was I doing with these?*)

(*They tremble.*)

H. ...

...

...

...

M. Daddy?

H. ...

M. Does it hurt?

Are you in –

H. No, I'm fine, Doodlebug.

(*Remembers.*)

(Continues working.)

H. But I won't be long.

The middle is always torture.

...

...

(Smiles.)

(Thinks this is darkly funny.)

That's prolly why ghosts always so damn pissed off in all those stories.

I been this way a day and already fallin' to ruin.

Those Victorian motherfuckers must be in some deep pain.

You think?

...

Littles?

...

...

Come on, now.

...

M. *(Refuses to joke about this.)* Leave me some long, I said.

...

...

(Stretches.)

Clotho. Lachesis. Atropos.

H. If you ever have children, you got names.

M. I do that,

They'll read a lot of Truman Capote.

H. You ever think of someday children?

You ever think of –

*(**M** gets up, picks up guitar, strums. Settles on playing the American traditional tune "Train on the Island.")*

That song –

M. Goes with the coat.

H. Don't go with you.

   You gonna listen? Littles –

M.

   TRAIN ON THE ISLAND, HEAR THE WHISTLE BLOW
   GO AND TELL MY OWN TRUE LOVE, I'M SICK AND I CAN'T
       GO

   TRAIN ON THE ISLAND, LISTEN TO HER SQUEAL
   GO AND TELL MY TRUE LOVE HOW HAPPY I DO FEEL

   I WENT OUT O'ER THE MOUNTAIN TO HEAR THAT BANJO
       RING,
   I WENT OUT O'ER THE OTHER SIDE JUST TO HEAR MY
       DARLING SING

   TRAIN ON THE ISLAND, WE'RE HEADED FOR THE EAST
   ME AND MY LOVE, WE DONE SPLIT UP, AND I AIN'T
       MISSING HIM IN THE LEAST, LEAST,
   AIN'T MISSIN' HIM IN THE LEAST.

   MAKE ME A BANJO OUT OF A GOURD AND STRING IT UP
       WITH TWINE
   THE ONLY TUNE THAT IT WOULD PLAY: "I WISH THAT
       MAN WERE MINE," MINE,
   I WISH THAT MAN WERE MINE.

   STILL I MISS MY DARLING, HE LEFT ME ALL ALONE
   THIS OLD HOUSE IS EMPTY; SILENT AS A STONE, STONE,
   SILENT AS A STONE.

   HEAR THE SOUND A-FAIDING OUT, I MISSED MY CHANCE
       AGAIN
   THE TRAIN'S ALREADY WEST OF TOWN AND THE BLUES
       ARE MOVING IN, IN,
   AND THE BLUES ARE MOVIN' IN.

   TRAIN ON THE ISLAND, HEAR THAT WHISTLE BLOW
   MAKES ME WANT TO PACK MY GRIP, HOP THAT FREIGHT
       AND GO, GO,
   HOP THAT FREIGHT AND GO.

       (We swing into an up-tempo instrumental
       version of the song.)

(H joins her on another instrument. They play together, fast and joyful for a few moments.)

(However, when she speeds up even faster, he has trouble following her lead.)

M. Come on, Daddy!

(H's hands ache, his body aches, he cannot play that fast anymore.)

(M realizes this.)

(H stops playing.)

(M stops as well.)

H. ...

I'll miss that of a morning.

M. *(Smiles.)* Ever bother you that her morning hymn,
Was a song of escape?

H. Not as long as we played it together.

M. She did get out though,
In the end, I guess.

H. She was troubled in a way nobody can fix, Littles.
You just live with what you're given.
If there's more on the way, well,
You just can't know.
But you got to try.

M. There's enough in standing still.
You found enough.

H. Your mother and I,
There was a time where I,

   ...

M. Love at first –

H. Before.
I'd lived all my life in the heat.
A child raised in fire.
Living with, above, life.
Skimming across the top.

The unwaking world.
There was the first time I saw her.
...
But there was a space of time,
From when I took my first breath,
To when I really started breathing.
That moment that usually lasts five seconds for ever'body else,
Lasted sixteen years for me.
I mean,
I knew how to get dressed,
And eat,
And sleep,
And lay fuses,
And diffuse the smell of gasoline.
I did do the, the things you do.
The waking life things.
But it was, mechanical,
A machine of a boy,
A machine of a man,
Not breathing. Not living.
There was a terrible completeness to it,
Which in the back of my mechanical mind equaled life.
A to B to C to D to E to F to end of day to end of night to end of morning to end of afternoon.
The completeness we're told makes you full, makes life life.
We'd weave and measure and cut and pretend to be the fates,
But really,
There was a coldness, Littles,
A chill that just, froze inside me, kept me from really breathing.
I'd stand in the warm afternoon rain not knowing why but craving the thaw.

The first time I touched her hand, pretending it was an
accident,
Brushed my fingers over hers at the market,
Reaching for a grocery bag,
I started gasping like a fish just reeled in on the boat.
I dropped to my knees and thought I was going to die.
Thought this is what it must feel like to be trapped in a
blaze that won't ever turn over and burn out. Thought
this is it.
The cut.
But she knelt down with me and took both my hands
and we breathed together.
And that was my first breath, Doodlebug,
My honest to God first.
And when we rose up together, I was a new man.
I was sixteen and just born and that was it.
I think you've been born, Littles, but you don't breathe.
You don't live like how your momma did for me.
You haven't started breathing yet.

M. She drove you and me to ends,
And then drove herself crazy.

H. There's something in that.
But there's also something beyond.
A fire in yourself so deep that you can't reach it without
someone else.

> (**M** *looks embarrassed.*)

I'm not talking about sex.
It's more intimate. A release, from yourself to yourself,
That takes someone else's love to ignite.
Otherwise you burn cold, no air, no breath, to feed the
flames,
Get you alive.
Clotho. Lachesis. Atropos.
That's your momma, Littles.
That's who your momma was to me.

Clotho – creator of my life.

Lachesis – measure of my life.

Atropos – my final destiny.

Now I'm going to go be with her,

You have to help me be with her.

And then you need to go off on your own.

Find your own breath, 'cause you haven't taken your first yet, Littles.

Not by any measure.

And you can't do that with me here.

Bury me whole and leave this place.

(Touches her coat.)

Lay down the burden of us; stop lettin' us bear you down.

M. …

…

…

…

…

I'm breathing, I am.

That's why I have you.

H. Oh, Doodlebug.

M. She pushed us.

H. Now –

M. We were,

Had to be,

A team. A little,

Almost twins just set apart in years.

H. You can't remember right.

When you find your –

M. I remember her crying when you'd go out at night.

The wails over the water, echoing off the trees.

The wanderings when I'd get out of bed and you'd both be gone.

And I'd curl up in your bed until one of you found your way back home.

H. There was plenty of other times too.

M. Why would I want that?

Why would I want that when I got this?

H. Times out on the boat,

Water picnic and sunset.

Times when she taught you to read, to write.

Times when you'd go to the store,

And she'd let you pick out the cans by color.

M. Time when I begged to go to school,

Like them other kids I saw,

And she feared the teachers would turn black and claw-footed,

And carry me away.

Like when she locked me up –

H. *(Has trouble remembering.)* That was only one time.

I think,

One time,

That I remember.

I think.

M. Not one time.

I remember,

Pressing darkness after pressing darkness after pressing darkness.

NEARER MY GOD TO THEE, NEARER TO THEE
NEARER MY GOD TO THEE, NEARER TO THEE

Like she's on repeat,

Stealing in through the cracks,

Like the smoke I smelled left on your curled hands,

When you'd come home in the morning,

And I'da been put back in bed.

Tucked in.

Like spending all night scrubbing the floor, wailin' an old hymn,

With your daughter locked in the closet wasn't crazy.

H. It was her sickness that made her special,

That healed me before.

That completeness that she broke and put back together,

Shard by shard,

So it was never complete but instead whole.

M. I know she didn't die like you said.

I know she wasn't sick, not really.

Not hospital sick. Not for doctors.

H. It don't matter –

M. The night before her funeral.

You ripping out yourself in the woods.

I sneaked over to the funeral home.

Crawled into the coffin.

I crawled in, all eight years slid between

The smooth velvet and her cold arm.

And I reached up to hold her face.

To give her a kiss and say I love you and I'm sorry and if I did this, if I did, if this was my fault, I'm sorry, it was probably my fault. It was probably my, because I was a,

Let's be truth now,

I was a

Pain in the ass.

And I's so sorry,

And to come on back home.

I'll be good.

But when I reached up to hold, to kiss,

I couldn't get to her face.

I couldn't because there wasn't no face there.

(Moves to stroke mother's face, but can't.)

There wasn't,

There was a chin,

And a mouth,

And a nose,

And bandages.
And I couldn't reach, or untie or unfold, or fold with or to or between us,
I couldn't,
I tried. I did.
I'm sorry, Momma, I'm trying but I can't reach you.
I never could. Not really.
And so I just snuggled down, held on to what was left,
And the next morning
The burial man find me
And he says,
"You can't be here young lady. You a bad young lady. Bad girl. Bad."
And he shoved me off.
But in that long last night, I held her.
I held her and I knew it was just gonna be me and you, Daddy.
Me and you, forever.
No one else.
No one else to cry or scream or,
...
Any of it.
Just us.
And now there are pieces missing from both of you.
And I don't want to find 'em.
Because it only means you'll go away.

H. ...
...
...
I'm sorry, Littles.
I wasn't, I shoulda...
...
...
It wasn't right, going off and leaving you that night.

M. It's not right to go off and leave me now.

H. I have to.

And you should move on.

You should –

M. I don't want that!

I don't want her,

Or a whatever she was to you!

I want you. I want you you

You you you you you

You you you.

> *(Pain hits **H** like a freight train. He groans.*
> *He strips off his shirt. There's scars, burnt*
> *skin, parched desert growing up the side of*
> *his body. Think: how Frida Kahlo would*
> *paint them. They are disturbing. They are*
> *beautiful.)*

H. This is where the pains come from, Littles.

Not being one or the other.

When I first rose up, there's nothing there.

Clean and strong, as if I's still alive.

Now, it grows.

It feeds on pain and memory,

And keeps growing.

I can't move on until you help me.

I can't stop this. I will fall apart.

You don't have me, Littles,

You think you do but it's like the tiger,

It's like the fire,

You can hold the tail a minute,

But in the end, it will bite you.

M. ...

...

...

...

(H *experiences another searing pain.*)

(M *exits.*)

(H *is left alone onstage.*)

H. ...

...

...

...

(H *is unsatisfied.*)

(*Most of the twine-fuse curtain is cut down. He checks the final lengths to see if they're dry.*)

(H *picks up the guitar, plays a bit of "Train on the Island."*)

(*It does not soothe him now.*)

(*He tries again. There is pain in his fingers.*)

(*The frustration and pain and lack of soothing builds.*)

(*Lights shift.*)

3. Outside Cabin

(**M** *stands outside the cabin at her mother's grave.*)

(*A song for* **M**'s *mother; American traditional hymn "Nearer My God to Thee."*)

M. (*A capella.*)

NEARER, MY GOD, TO THEE, NEARER TO THEE!
EVEN THOUGH IT BE A CROSS THAT RAISETH ME,
STILL ALL MY SONG SHALL BE, NEARER MY GOD, TO THEE.
NEARER, MY GOD, TO THEE, NEARER TO THEE!

THOUGH LIKE THE WANDERER, THE SUN GONE DOWN,
DARKNESS BE OVER ME, MY REST A STONE;
YET IN MY DREAMS I'D BE NEARER, MY GOD, TO THEE.
NEARER, MY GOD, TO THEE, NEARER TO THEE!

THERE IN MY FATHER'S HOME, SAFE AND AT REST,
THERE IN MY SAVIOR'S LOVE, PERFECTLY BLEST;
AGE AFTER AGE TO BE NEARER, MY GOD, TO THEE.
NEARER, MY GOD, TO THEE, NEARER TO THEE!

I hope that calms your nerves, Momma,
Calms so you can really hear me.
Prolly don't need calming now though.
Anyways,
I just came to say,
He'll be there soon.
I'm supposed to collect...

...

Don't matter.

...

He'll be at your front door.
You will have your god back.
All loving, all forgiving.
Stories of tigers an' all.

(Removes her mother's coat, lays it on the grave. A moment of prayer and a sign of grace.)

M. …

I've got to go…

(Doesn't want to go.)

But did you know, Momma?
Did you know that even the gods
Were made to bow
To Clotho, Lachesis, and Atropos.
On knee and forehead,
Like the tallest pine in the hurricane,
Bent low in the dirt.

…

Clotho. Lachesis. Atropos.
Cousin Need made me say their names again and again
Until I had them straight, right from beginning to
ending.
An invocation.
Clotho.
The old Greek lady who wove the thread of life.
Lachesis.
The old Greek lady who measured the thread of life.
Atropos.
The Old Greek lady who cut the thread of life.
"The three who decided," Cousin Need said.
'Cause that's the real power, Momma.
The true glory from age to age.
The deciding and everyone having to listen.
To follow.
To bow.
That kinda power isn't fit for us humans.
That's why we fuck it up so much.
We falsify the testament,

They are the word.

We obfuscate.

They make clear and certain.

"Don't confuse appearance with the real thing," Need said.

I guess we're just askin' for trouble,

Us with our clean knees,

Not goin' down in the dirt for nobody,

Pretendin' we don't bend in the wind.

...

Was it the weight of the pretendin' that killed you, Momma?

The burden of...

I've been cutting and lighting and left cold by the fire now,

And I think he's right.

We're just frayed silhouettes of those ladies,

That's the best we can be.

Maybe you done it right, Momma,

Cutting the threads yourself.

You took control but look where it got you.

And Daddy and I trying to be mightier than the gods

And this is what we all come to.

...

To cut the twine.

Ain't none of us fit for it.

...

I know what I gotta do.

But I wish you were here to tell me that I don't have to do it.

...

Please tell me,

I can just stay here in the dark with you,

Just a bit longer.

Your Littles again.
We'll just sit here quiet, okay?
Just sit,
Just –

H. *(From cabin.)* Littles!

M. *(Lays on ground.)* If I lay here in the dark,
Will you tell on me, Momma?
I laid all night with you once.

H. *(From cabin, confused and in pain.)* Littles, you there?
I forget,

...

Littles?

...

The...

    (Sound of pain.)

Damn it!
I can't remember what you look like.
I need to,
I need you, Littles.
You are stronger than me.
I love you.

    *(**M** can no longer avoid his pain. Exits.)*
    (Lights shift.)

4. Cabin

(**H** *sits, the guitar across his lap.*)

(**H** *is keeping his pain under control.*)

(**M** *appears at the door, enters.*)

(*She carries a small bag covered in soot, a little blood soaking through. It holds the rest of him. Sits on the opposite side of the room from him.*)

M. ...

   ...

   ...

   ...

      (*For a while.*)

   ...

H. When you were first born,
   Squalling, by the bedside,
   The world that was so big got so little.
   So fast.
   Ever'one of my breaths
   Could fit inside your tiny hand.
   You had me from then, Littles.

M. (*Cannot bring herself to look at him.*) ...

   ...

   ...

      (**H** *begins to strum the guitar.*)

      (*Quotes the original myth:*)

H.

   BUT LATER HE WILL SUFFER WHATEVER FATE
   SPUN FOR HIM WITH HER THREAD AT HIS BIRTH
   WHEN HIS MOTHER BORE HIM

   ...

(He stops playing.)

H. We are measured and fit for something at birth,
    Just takes a little time
    To spin itself out.

    ...

    I don't know, Littles.
    But when,
    From that first time,
    When you grabbed my breath
    To this right now,
    I'm not ashamed of nothin'.
    Not bothered by,
    Any of it.
    I know that when you turn,
    I will turn,
    When you breathe,
    I breathe,
    When you go –

        (She finally looks at him.)

    I go with you.
    ...

    Cinched deep in your bones.
    In the spaces between,
    Like the air between the threads of twine that lets fire
    grow.
    No matter how short or long it's cut,
    How much is released,
    I am in you and you in me.
    That's the whole of it.

M. ...

    ...

    ...

...

(**M** *walks over to him, hands him the bag.*)

...

...

...

H. ...

...

...

(**M** *reaches up, touches his head like she touched her mother's in the coffin.*)

(**M** *gives* **H** *a kiss on the cheek.*)

(**H** *leaves the guitar, slips back down into the hole with his bag, the way he came.*)

M. ...

...

...

...

(*She leans over the hole. Touches her fingers to her lips, kisses them, touches her fingers to the hole. A moment of prayer, a sign of grace.*)

(*She is lost.*)

(**M** *looks around, sees the last few remaining twine fuses hanging from the ceiling, touches them. They are now dry.*)

(**M** *begins to measure and cut.*)

(*The sound of a tiger roaring in the distance.*)

(**M** *stops.*)

(*She lets the fuses hang.*)

(*She lights a match, tosses it into the hole after her father.*)

(*She looks around one final time as the house burns.*)

(Picks up the guitar, but nothing else, and moves on.)

(She exits.)

End of Play